The T-Rex who Lost his Specs!

Jeanne Willis

Tony Ross

ANDERSEN PRESS

There was a T-Rex who lost his specs
and got himself in trouble.

Everything seemed very blurred
and sometimes he saw...

He did not recognise his clothes
when he was getting dressed...

... so put his sister's knickers on
and wore his granny's vest.

He went to give himself a wash
but could not find the basin...

... and so the toilet was the place
that T-Rex washed his face in.

Then when he went to dry himself,
he thought he'd grabbed a towel...

... but rubbed himself all over
with a prehistoric owl.

He went to make his breakfast
but believing they were kippers...

... he fried and ate his brother's sock
and toasted Grandpa's slippers.

And as it was a windy day
he went to fetch his kite.

But as he could not find the string
he tied a new one, tight.

Although the kite put up a fight,
he dragged it through the door,
not realising that it was...

... a GIANT pterosaur!

Convinced its cries were just the wind,
the T-Rex climbed the hill...

... in fact a brontosaurus
who was lying very still!

The 'hill' stood up! The 'kite' took off!
What happened to T-Rex?

Some like to think he is extinct
because he lost his specs.

In truth, his best friends saved him but because he could not see,
he thought he had been captured by an evil enemy.

So T-Rex ate them, one by one, and being in a muddle,
he ran to mum but...

... gave his *real* enemy a cuddle!